Dealing with JEALOUSY

Learning to manage ENVY

Jasmine Brooke

FOX EYE
PUBLISHING

Sometimes, Panther could be **JEALOUS**. He could be **ENVIOUS** of others.

If a friend received a present,
Panther wanted it for himself.
If someone else won a prize,
Panther was not **HAPPY**.
He wanted the prize instead.

Feeling so very **JEALOUS**
and being so **ENVIOUS**
could be a problem for Panther.

On Monday, Mrs Tree said that everyone could play a musical instrument in the show. Bear would play the guitar and Tiger the piano. Monkey would play the drums and Panther would play the triangle.

But Panther would rather have played the guitar or, even better, the drums.

Panther felt **JEALOUS** and **ENVIOUS** of everyone.

"Well done!" Mrs Tree smiled as everyone played. Everyone except Panther.

Mrs Tree called to Panther and told him it was his turn to play. But Panther didn't want to play the triangle. He scowled and frowned with **ENVY** as he stared at everyone.

Then, **CROSSLY**, Panther BANGED his triangle! "Hmm," said Mrs Tree. "Maybe next time, play a little more gently."

Next, Mrs Tree said that everyone could have a singing role. Tiger would sing first, then Monkey, Wolf and Gorilla. “You can sing at the very end and steal the show!” she told Panther.

But Panther would rather have been first. He was not pleased at all.

Panther felt **JEALOUS** and **ENVIOUS** of everyone.

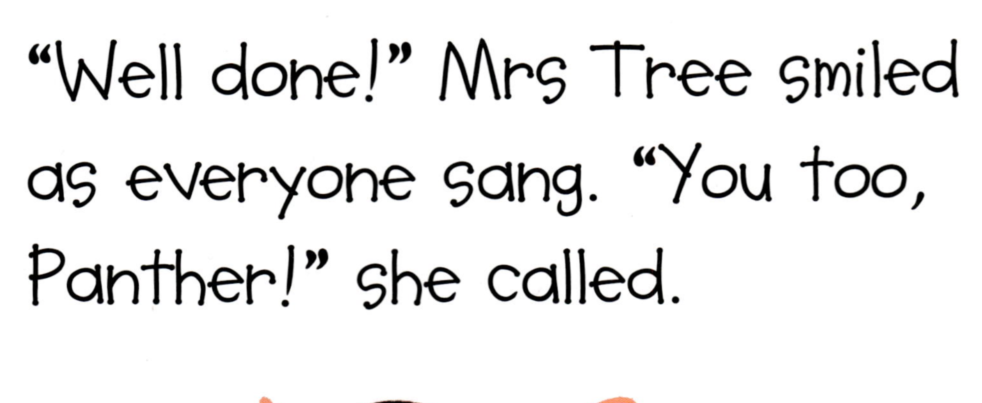

"Well done!" Mrs Tree smiled as everyone sang. "You too, Panther!" she called.

But Panther scowled
and frowned with **ENVY**
as he stared at everyone.
Then, **ANGRILY**, Panther
ROARED his song. "Hmm,"
said Mrs Tree. "Next time,
maybe less **ANGRILY**."

Next, it was time to put on costumes. Zebra would be a flower. Peacock and Cheetah would be bees and Giraffe would be a very tall tree. “Panther will be the sun,” Mrs Tree said, “so he can shine on everyone!”

But Panther would rather have been a bee. Or even a tree. He was not pleased at all.

Panther felt **JEALOUS**. He felt so **ENVIOUS** of everyone.

Mrs Tree could see that Panther was not pleased. "What's wrong?" she kindly asked. "I don't want to be the sun!" shouted Panther. "I feel **JEALOUS** of everyone!"

Then Mrs Tree smiled, "Feeling **ENVIOUS** is no fun. Try to feel happy with what you have – it's a far nicer way to be."

Now, Panther had to agree –
feeling **JEALOUS** was no fun!

So Panther played his triangle and sang so beautifully, and in his sun costume at the front of the stage, Panther danced happily – outshining everyone!

Then Panther realised he didn't mind not being a bee. He didn't even want to be a tree. Panther had learnt that ...

feeling **HAPPY** felt far better than **JEALOUSY**.

Words and feelings

Panther felt very jealous in this story. He often felt envious and that made him feel unhappy.

JEALOUSY

ENVY

There are a lot of words to do with jealousy and learning to be happy in this book. Can you remember all of them?

Let's talk about behaviour

This series helps children to understand and manage difficult emotions and behaviours. The animal characters in the series have been created to show human behaviour that is often seen in young children, and which they may find difficult to manage.

Dealing with Jealousy

The story in this book examines issues around feeling jealous and dealing with envy. It looks at how feeling jealous of others stops people feeling good about themselves and their own situations. Jealousy also damages relationships with others.

The book is designed to show young children how they can manage their behaviour and overcome envy.

How to use this book

You can read this book with one child or a group of children. The book can be used to begin a discussion around complex behaviour such as learning to overcome jealousy.

The book is also a reading aid, with enlarged and repeated words to help children to develop their reading skills.

How to read the story

Before beginning the story, ensure that the children you are reading to are relaxed and focused.

Take time to look at the enlarged words and the illustrations, and discuss what this book might be about before reading the story.

New words can be tricky for young children to approach. Sounding them out first, slowly and repeatedly, can help children to learn the words and become familiar with them.

How to discuss the story

When you have finished reading the story, use these discussion points and questions to examine the theme of the story with children and explore the emotions within it:

- What do you think the story was about? Have you been in a situation in which you felt jealous? What was that situation? For example, did a friend get a prize that you wanted for yourself? Encourage the children to talk about their experiences.
- Talk about ways that people can learn to overcome feelings of jealousy. For example, think about how it might feel to be happy for a friend if they win a prize, rather than focusing on feeling envy. Talk to the children about what tools they think might work for them and why.
- Discuss what it is like to be jealous. Explain that because Panther was jealous all the time, he did not enjoy experiences and find happiness in his own achievements.
- Talk about why it is important to overcome jealousy and learn to be content with your own experiences and achievements. Explain that by feeling happy for others who achieve, you in turn will feel far happier with your own circumstances.

Titles in the series

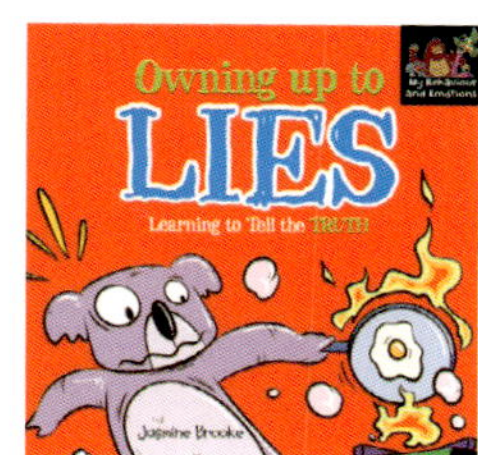

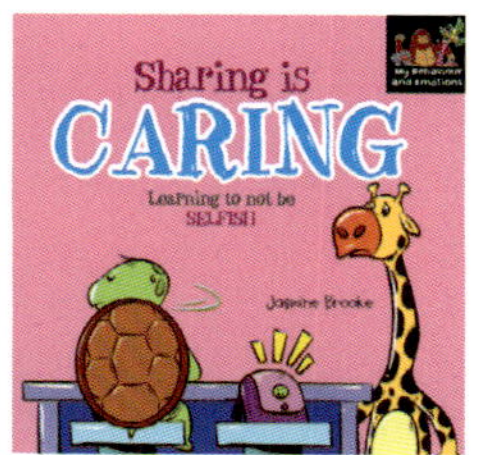

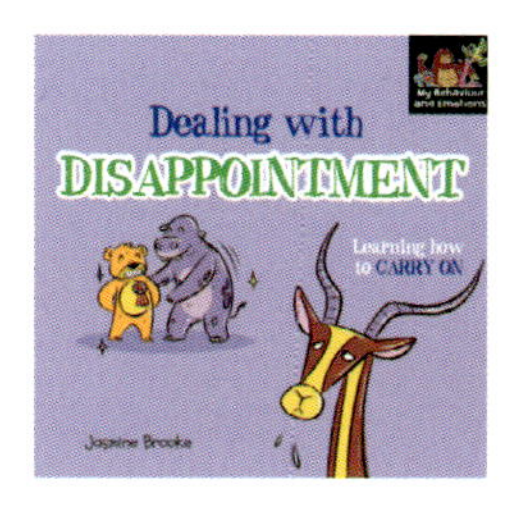

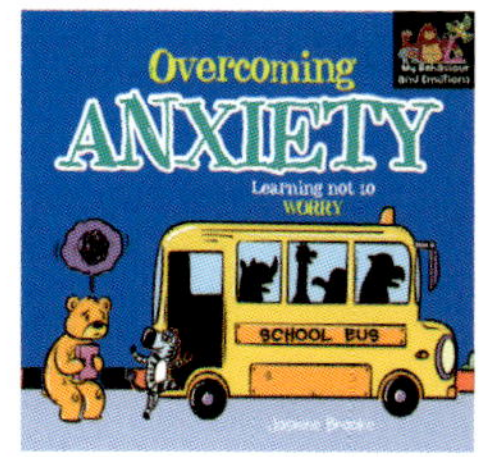

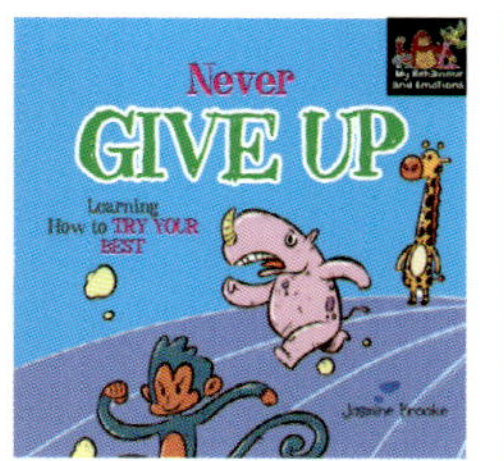

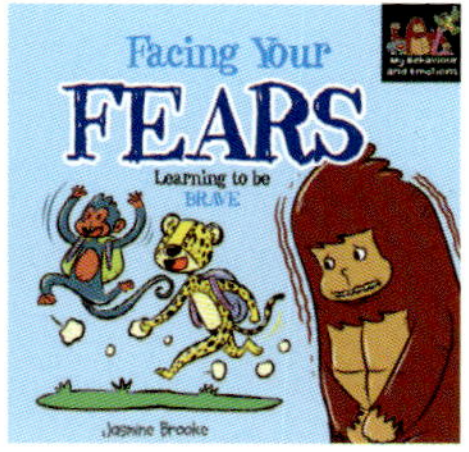

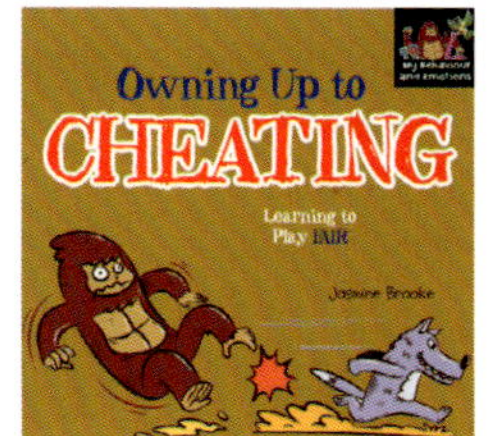

First published in 2023 by Fox Eye Publishing
Unit 31, Vulcan House Business Centre,
Vulcan Road, Leicester, LE5 3EF
www.foxeyepublishing.com

Author: Jasmine Brooke
Art director: Paul Phillips
Cover designer: Emma Bailey & Salma Thadha
Editor: Jenny Rush

All illustrations by Novel

ISBN 978-1-80445-302-5

A catalogue record for this book is available from the British Library

Printed in China